# Egyptian Diary

For my sister, Julie
**R. P.**

For the staff and children of St. Faith and St. Martin CE Junior School
**D. P.**

Text copyright © 2005 by Richard Platt
Illustrations copyright © 2005 by David Parkins

First U.S. paperback edition 2014

The Library of Congress has cataloged the hardcover edition as follows:

Platt, Richard.
Egyptian diary : the journal of Nakht / Richard Platt ; illustrated by David Parkins. — 1st U.S. ed.
Parkins, David, ill.
Summary: In ancient Egypt, Nakht records his experiences as his family moves from small town
Esna to the big, exciting city of Memphis, where he studies to be a scribe like his father and helps
discover who has been robbing graves. Includes nonfiction information about Egyptian culture.
ISBN 978-0-7636-2756-0 (hardcover)
[1. Scribes — Egypt — Fiction. 2. Grave robbing — Fiction. 3. Diaries — Fiction. 4. Memphis
(Extinct city) — History — Fiction. 5. Egypt — Civilization–To 332 B.C.—Fiction.]
I. Title.
PZ7.P71295Eg 2005
[Fic] — dc22        2005046911

ISBN 978-0-7636-7054-2 (paperback)

19 20 21 22 23 MNG 10 9 8 7 6 5

Printed in Saline, MI, U.S.A.

This book was typeset in Truesdell and ITC Braganza.
The illustrations were done in watercolor and ink.

Candlewick Press
99 Dover Street
Somerville, Massachusetts 02144

visit us at www.candlewick.com

# Egyptian Diary

## THE JOURNAL OF

## Nakht,

### YOUNG SCRIBE

## RICHARD PLATT

## *illustrated by* DAVID PARKINS

CANDLEWICK PRESS

# This Is the Journal of
# Nakht of Esna
# in the Eighth Year of
# King Hatshepsut

**Y**ESTERDAY I begged from Father the new roll on which I now set down these words. I want to write down everything that happens, that I might forget nothing. For our lives are about to change, and very soon. The god Khnum has smiled upon us and blessed us with extreme good luck! My uncle's uncle (a man I have never met) has written to us. He is a scribe in the great city of Memphis. He discovered that lesser officials have been cutting the taxes of farmers who bribed them. To reward him for his honesty and cleverness, the king has given him great power. Now this man summons Father to work for him in Memphis. Father will still be a scribe, as he is now, but his work will be much more important. So in a month, we leave our little house in dusty, dull Esna and take the boat to the city. Our journey will take ten days or more. Father left this morning, so I have a holiday from his lessons, but he will teach me again to be a scribe when we join him in Memphis.

My older sister, Tamyt, says that moving down the river to a grand house bores her. However, I do not believe her, for she has begun to act very grand among her friends. She also braids flowers in her hair as if she is a princess.

I must stop now, for my brush wears out. Tomorrow I will make a new one, and I will have more to write about our new life.

## Nineteenth day of the first month of the season of Flood

This morning, the star Sopdet reappeared at dawn,

marking the start of the New Year. Officially it is the first proper day of the flood season. However, the great river changed its color to green ten days ago, and this is always a sign that the flood has begun.

## Twentieth day

We have so little time to prepare for our journey! I spent this morning packing with Tamyt and Mother. There is room on the boat only for food, the clothes we need for the trip, our most valued possessions, and just one servant. We will take Ahmose; Neshi will pack what remains and bring it when he follows later.

## Twenty-fourth day

This afternoon, we went to the seamstress, for Mother says our old tunics will look out of place in the smart city. She will have new clothes too and must now get used to wearing leather shoes! She has two pairs:

both hurt her feet, and she kicks them off as soon as she steps into the house. But in Memphis (Tamyt tells me), only poor people and servants wear shoes made of reed.

## Last day

Today we began our journey to Memphis. We wanted to leave before the sun rose, when it was still cool, but Myt delayed us. She was nowhere to be seen when we were ready to go, though we looked in every room. We eventually found her hiding behind a bundle of mats, her ears back and her tail beating the air. To calm her, we gave her some beer and coaxed her into a basket for the journey.

Then we set off. Neshi carried our luggage to the jetty with help from some of our neighbors. Ahmose went on ahead to tell the boatmen we were delayed. Our friends in the town delayed us even longer. All came out to wish us a good trip. They gave us honey cakes, beer, and fruit from their orchards: "Just in case you get hungry," they said. By the time we reached the river, we had enough food for half the trip!

The current was flowing so quickly that we loaded and boarded our boat with some trouble, but at last we were under way. Pulling on their oars, our boatmen moved us to the center of the stream, where the water is deepest and the flow strongest. In just a few moments, we were around the bend in the river, and the crowd waving from the jetty vanished behind the hills. When will we see our friends again?

## Second day of the second month of flood

Yesterday I wrote nothing, for there was so much to see. And now that I have time to write, I find it is not as easy on water as it is on land: the scroll wobbles in my lap! We passed through Thebes just before noon yesterday. Its City of the Dead, where the great kings of Egypt are buried, stands on the left bank. It was impossible to see any of the tombs, but near the river there are beautiful gardens. Beyond them, new buildings line the bank. The sun sparkled so brilliantly off their white painted walls that I could gaze at them for only a moment before covering my eyes.

When we drew closer, it was my nose I had to protect, for on the other side of the river, a stinking jumble of buildings fills the valley. The edges of the city are not so bad, for there are many fine houses and gardens. But in its center, it looks as if someone took twenty towns like Esna and threw them together in a heap. Some houses are stacked one on top of another, two or even three high. People swarmed over everything — even the water itself — like flies on a dead dog! They stood in small boats so close together that our ship was surrounded. Each boatman had something to sell. They shouted so loudly that I took my hand from my nose to cover my ears.

To escape, our captain yelled to our boatmen, and

they leaned hard on their oars. Soon we had left behind the glittering City of the Dead and the stinking town of the living.

After being on the boat all day, I felt sticky, hot, and tired when at last we moored. As soon as we had tied up, one of our boatmen went off hunting. By the time a fire was burning, he had returned with enough duck and fish to make a meal for us all. We slept aboard the boat and men from the local village guarded us. They sat up all night warming themselves by the flames of a brushwood fire.

## Third day

Our boat is not the fastest on the water nor the slowest. We pass lumbering barges, laden with huge blocks of stone, on their way to build fine temples. But we could never keep pace with the slim boats of the king's messengers. They race past us, pushed not only by the current but also by teams of boatmen at their oars.

## Eleventh day

Our country is like the long thin stem of a lotus plant.
We have been sailing down it for ten days, yet in all that
time the river valley was no wider than an hour's walk —
often much less.

Yesterday, though, the river valley widened on the left
bank, until the fields stretched so far I could no longer
see the desert.

The river is now dark red, which the boatmen say is
the blood of Osiris, god of the dead. However, it looks
just like mud to me.

## Twelfth day

Today (at last) we came in sight of Memphis. Tamyt
spotted it before me; she pointed and shouted, "Look!
the White Walls!" I saw at once why this was the city's
old name. Its walls are almost as high as date palms and
shine brighter than the feathers of an ibis. Beyond and
to the left of the city are the famous pyramids of Saqqara.

Before Father left, I made him promise
he would take us to see them, as well as Khufu's pyramid
at Giza — which is even bigger, and only half a day's
travel across the edge of the desert. When we neared the
dockside, a boy waved to us, and the boatmen threw him
the mooring rope. As soon as he had tied it fast, he ran
to fetch Father, who led us into the city.

# Fourteenth day

Our new house on the edge of the city is much bigger than our home at Esna, and I like it much better. It stands in a garden, shaded by tall date palms. Although the desert is just outside the garden wall, trees can grow because the house is built on land only a little above the river. Their roots reach down to drink the river water.

Our front door opens in a very unusual way. A bolt keeps the door shut, and the only way to draw it back is to slide a specially shaped stick into a hole in the door and lift it. Without the stick, nobody can enter the house.

The house has many rooms, the grandest of which is a hall, with four tall tree trunks holding up the ceiling. There are no doors or windows on the side that faces the hot noon sun; most are on the other side to catch the cool wind when it blows. There are wind vents in the roof too.

Best of all, though, I have my OWN BEDROOM, so

I do not have to share with Tamyt anymore. My wall is painted with a hunting scene.

## Sixteenth day

Yesterday, carpenters brought a bed for me. It is made of a web of woven cords, which are soft to lie upon. At the end of the day, I crept between the cool linen sheets and lay down.

Yet no matter which way I lay, sleep did not come. I thought perhaps I had offended the sun god, Amun-Re, and I tried moving the bed so that my head faced the rising sun. Eventually I gave up and put my old mat and headrest on the floor as I am used to, and instantly fell asleep!

## Twenty-fifth day

Today I tasted ox meat. When we lived in Esna, the priests would sometimes give us parts of an ox they had sacrificed to please the gods. But it was always the heart (which was disgusting) or the tail (which I did not want to eat, for I knew where it had hung). However, now that Father is more important, he can barter for the leg of an ox. It was delicious, and made more so by our new cook, who boiled it in a stew with figs.

## Third day of the third month of flood

Tomorrow I start my studies again, but not with Father. Here at Memphis, there is a school for scribes, where I must learn with other boys. To mark the start of school, Tamyt gave me a new palette. My old one was of cheap wood, but this is carved from fine stone. It has two blocks of ink to mix into a paste with water, so now I can write in both black *and* red. As soon as she gave it to me,

I took a new reed and chewed the end thoroughly into a fine brush, which I am using to write these words.

## Fifth day

The school is on the other side of town, so I have a long walk to reach it. We study all morning beneath a huge tree, but by noon it becomes too hot to work even in this shade, and our classes end.

I had hoped that studying with other boys would be more interesting, but I was wrong. It's EVEN WORSE! Most of the exercises we do are EXACTLY the same as those I did with Father in Esna a year past.

We even study in the same way. Today our teacher chanted that rhyme from *Kemit* about how wonderful it is to be a scribe:

*"Be a scribe, for he controls everyone;*

*He who works in writing pays no taxes . . ."*

and so on. We had to chant it back to him — just as I did at home — then copy it down.

A few things are new: we are learning not only the everyday kind of writing but also the old hieroglyphic picture letters that are needed for temple walls and grand public inscriptions.

There is another different thing. At home I used to write on broken pieces of pottery, just as Father did for quick notes not worth a square of papyrus. But at school, we use slivers of stone instead. When they are full, we scrape off the writing and use them again.

I have made a friend at school: Ptahmay, whom everyone just calls May. He is the same age as me, but more cunning: he has helped me escape a beating once already.

## Twelfth day

This afternoon we all went to the temple to see the Nilometer and celebrate the festival of Hapy, the river god.

Since it is an important festival, the Controller of

Granaries was there. This man has clean, smooth hands and a big belly, so it was clear that he does not *really* measure out the grain, for it would keep him fit and make him very dusty. Father grinned when I said this to him. He told me that the Controller is in charge of all the granaries around Memphis and much else as well. I judged him to be VERY important, for he wears not only a pleated shirt that matches his kilt but also bracelets, a fancy wig, a large ring, and a gold collar.

The flood has reached its greatest height — it came within ten steps of the Nilometer. This staircase has grooves cut into its steps to measure the water level exactly. With this knowledge, the Controller of Granaries can estimate how great the harvest will be (for the wetter the mud, the more grain grows) and so set the taxes for next year.

I threw a pebble into the water of the Nilometer to see the ripples, but the splash was louder than I thought possible. When we got home, I was beaten for my lack of respect for Hapy.

## Thirteenth day

School today would have been as dull as usual if not for Thutmose, who had captured a large beetle. He glued one end of a long thread to its tail, and held the other one. We were chanting:

> "Be a scribe, who is free
> of forced labor,
> and protected from all
> heavy work. . . ."

when we all heard a low buzzing above our heads. Looking up, we saw that

Thutmose's beetle had taken wing, but because of the thread, it could fly only in circles. Our teacher, spying the insect, set it free, then beat Thutmose with a hippopotamus-hide whip. The rest of us had to write out ten times on our stones:

*The ear of a boy is on his back,*
*for he only listens when he is beaten.*

## Twentieth day

Yesterday evening we heard chanting and wailing and guessed a funeral was passing.

Tamyt and I climbed on the garden wall to watch. It was a good one — bigger than any I had seen before. At the front of the procession were dancers. Behind them came a crowd of women dressed in pale clothes and covered in dust. They tugged at their hair and yelled in sorrow. (Mother later told me that they are paid to mourn the dead. Tomorrow they will sob just as loudly for another stranger.) Behind *them* came a great crowd

of servants carrying supplies for the tomb. There was enough food and drink for a banquet, as well as great heaps of clothes, many jars, boxes, and even furniture. Tamyt, who has a sharp eye, whispered that some of the furniture looked a little scuffed, and surely the dead man deserved better. The ceremony at the tomb would bring him back to life, she said, and his chair and bed would need to last him for eternity. One man held a palette and brushes, so we guessed a scribe had died. Sure enough, when a priest passed by us carrying a statue of the dead man, it showed him cross-legged with a scroll on his lap, ready to write.

After this came another priest, wearing a panther skin, and at last the coffin itself, pulled on a sled by oxen. It was VERY grand and painted in brilliant colors. A priestess walked behind it, dressed in feathers as the hawk goddess Isis.

Seeing a crowd of children running behind the procession, we jumped down and joined them. We would have followed right the way to the tomb at Saqqara too, but we were chased away by a young priest after some of the children joined the chanting like an echo. This was a shame, for I wanted to see if a dead man really *does* come back to life when the priest carries out the ceremony. For if the dead do live again, why do they seal them in tombs?

## First day of the fourth month of flood

The river level is beginning to go down, but if we travel beyond the city walls, we still have to go by boat. It will be some time before the ground is dry enough to walk on.

Tamyt and I found a reed boat floating at the river's edge. We made paddles from palm leaves and rowed to an island a little way downstream. We have hidden the boat among reeds and plan to make more voyages together!

## Seventh day

At school, we began our studies of great building and engineering. First we calculated how to move the huge blocks of stone used to build temples. (I know nothing of this, for Father is concerned more with harvests and crops than with stone blocks.)

We could find the weight of each block by copying equations that our teacher gave us and replacing his numbers with new ones. In this way, we worked out how much a stone needle would weigh. Then we were asked to calculate how many men would be needed to move it — and how much food and drink to allow them during their work. At least May was able to do these things, but I was not, so I copied what he had written.

## Fifteenth day

This day a scorpion stung Tamyt. We had returned to our island and Tamyt must have disturbed a stone under which the scorpion was sleeping. The creature, being suddenly awoken, was irritable (as Father is when he awakes after drinking palm wine) and stung her. Luckily it was a black scorpion and she was able to limp home. I have seen a pale one sting a dog: it fell to the ground and could not rise for a day and a night.

## Twenty-third day

May and I were beaten today because May was no better than I at guessing the weight of stones. When I copied his work, I also copied his mistakes.

We learned this morning some of the secrets of the engineer. Our teacher took us out into the fields around the city and asked us, "How would you dig the canal so that the river water reaches as many fields as possible?"

It was a difficult question and (it's true) an important one. Little rain falls, and the crops would not grow without water from the river. Though we all puzzled at the problem, none of us could find a solution. Yet the answer, when our teacher told us, is simple. The slope of the canal must be *just* steep enough for the water to flow away from the river, but no steeper. If it is too steep, the water does not flow far enough and its force washes away the canal sides. But if it is too gentle, the water flows too slowly and weeds grow, blocking the canal.

As we returned, we stopped to watch a farmer water his field. He kicked a hole in the earth bank of the canal, and when the water had flooded one plot, he plugged the hole with mud. Then he did the same to flood the next plot. The farmer waved at us and shouted, "This is what they call 'watering with your foot!'"

This evening Father told us that the tomb of the scribe who was buried last month has been robbed. The thieves stole everything made of gold and other precious objects. To reach the underground burial room, they had to lower themselves down a deep shaft, then burrow through rubble that filled a long tunnel leading to the coffin. It must have taken many nights — and yet the soldiers who guard the City of the Dead noticed nothing!

## Last day of the season of flood

At last, I am a scribe! Well, not quite, though I swear by Thoth that I soon shall be! Yesterday, when I returned from my studies, Father sent for me. "You learn much at school," he told me, "but you will learn even more with me, and besides, you can make yourself useful." So, beginning tomorrow, I will spend my mornings at school as usual and my afternoons following him, as if I were his shadow. He also plans to arrange for me to follow other scribes so that I can see all the work that they do.

Hearing this, I begged Father to cut off my sidelock. If I am to work like a man, why should I still look like a boy? Alas, he refused.

## First day of the first month of the season of Planting

As this was the first day of the season of planting, Father took me with him out into the fields, where he inspects the work of the surveyor scribes.

These scribes copy the exact shapes of the fields on papyrus, on a much smaller scale. In this way, when the flood goes down, they settle arguments about the sizes of fields. The river mud that makes our land so fertile also hides the boundaries between fields. The large stones that mark the field corners show through the mud, but by moving a stone a cubit each year, a farmer can steal his neighbor's land little by little.

Though it is traditional for the surveyors to measure land today, it was really too early, and the ground was like a marsh. To carry out their duties, they had to wallow in mud and soon became covered in it. In the sun, the mud peeled off in patches, so that some of the men looked like oxen.

## Twentieth day

I did not go out with Father this afternoon, for he is again concerned with a tomb robbery. Instead, I went swimming in the river with May and other friends from school. We had to sneak away secretly to do this, for each of us has been forbidden from diving in deep water. Our parents say it is dangerous unless one of them is with us.

May brought his dog and tied it up nearby. The water was deliciously cool, but we sprang out when we heard a commotion of splashing and barking. A wily crocodile had seen the dog drinking and snapped it up in his enormous jaws.

Having lost the dog,
we all had to admit our narrow
escape when we got home, and each of us was beaten.
It was not for the loss of the dog (which May's father
considers an offering to the crocodile god, Sobek), but
for our disobedience.

## Twenty-first day

On the way to school today, I heard oxen lowing far
from the marshes where they usually graze. In the sky,

hundreds of birds circled, screaming almost as loudly as the herd below were mooing. I went to see what could be the cause of such a racket.

It was the farmers planting seed corn. As they scattered it, their children walked behind, shooing away the birds, but still many swooped down to peck at the seeds. Their feast continued until the farmers called on the herdsmen to whip their oxen across the field and stomp the seeds into the mud.

The herdsmen were easy to pick out: They stood apart, and had stubbly chins and shaven heads. They appeared awkward in their badly tied loincloths and spoke little. Alone in the wetlands, they need no clothes and have only their beasts and the fish for company.

## Twenty-third day

I came home from school yesterday along the river. Moored at the wharf were several big ships of a kind new to me. Unlike riverboats, these ships were plain at the back, instead of having carved rear posts. One was filled with logs. The others carried cargoes of jars.

On the nearest ship was a boy of about my age. He did not wear his hair in a sidelock, so I guessed he was foreign. When I walked past, he greeted me with an insult so rude that I dare not write it down. However, he smiled as he shouted, so I smiled back and asked him how he knew our language. "Because I speak ALL languages," he replied, and cursed me in five more ways, each one different.

He said he had sailed from the port of Byblos with his two brothers. They had a cargo of oil and wine, which they would barter here in Memphis for grain and linen.

He pulled me onto the ship by my arm and, pouring us both a sweet drink from a jar, he told me how he had learned so many ways of talking. From Byblos, he has sailed toward the setting sun, to the island of Crete and beyond. Besides cedar and pine, his ship has carried lapis lazuli, silver, copper sheets shaped like cowhides, ostrich eggs, amber, amethyst, and fine stone to flake into shaving blades.

After we had taken another drink, his eyes grew wilder and he told me of sea monsters he had killed with his bare hands, of exploding hills that belched fire and smoke, and of how he had escaped from pirates. As I remember no more after this, I must have fallen asleep.

I awoke at dusk and found myself lying on the riverbank. The ships had gone. So, too, had my palette and brushes. Then, when I got to my feet, I found that my legs would not work properly and I had trouble getting home.

When I arrived, Father sent me to bed, saying, "I will beat you tomorrow, when you will feel it more keenly."

However, when I awoke this morning, I felt that there were stonemasons in my head, using their chisels to get out. Father decided this was punishment enough.

## Twenty-fifth day

Father announced that he is to visit Saqqara tomorrow. He has already been there with the scribes who are looking into the robberies from the tombs, but now he wishes to return alone — for, as he says, "With the scribes nearby, I suspect that I see only what they want me to see." Tamyt and I begged to go with him, for we have never been to this great city of tombs. At first he said no, but our begging wore him down.

## First day of the second month of Planting

Our trip to Saqqara nearly landed Tamyt and me in jail!

And it is only now — three days later — that I dare write down what happened.

When we reached the City of the Dead, I was disappointed. Though the biggest pyramid (Djoser's) is tall and impressive, the other three are small and dull. We passed by quickly because a strong breeze from the desert was whipping up the sand and stinging our legs. There was more shelter among the other tombs, which surround the bigger pyramids like buildings in a town.

All the robbed tombs seemed alike, so after we had seen the first few with father, Tamyt and I began to chase each other through the narrow alleys between them. We enjoyed this game so much that we did not notice the breeze becoming a storm. By then, all we could do was find shelter. Sand choked and half blinded us and matted our hair. We crept through a doorway and huddled together.

After what seemed like hours, the wind died down. I could smell smoke and saw that flickering flames lit up the painted walls of the tomb where we were sheltering. Four men stood around a ladder that led down to the underground burial chambers. They were gathering up beautiful jewelry and golden decorations broken off from furniture. I heard one hiss, "Hurry! We have been too long. The moon is high. It is near the time we told the guards to come."

Tamyt and I scurried to the darkest corner so they would not see us. When the men slunk past our hiding place, Tamyt shrank back, and I saw why when I followed her eyes. A torch lit up the hand of the man carrying it, and he had only three fingers! On one finger was a gold ring engraved with signs.

I glimpsed the ring for just a moment before they hurried off into the night. When they had gone, I ran to the ladder and started to climb down. Tamyt called, "Nakht! No!" but then she climbed down after me. A sweet smell filled the tunnel, and the glow from tiny lamps led away to where it forked. Tamyt grabbed me

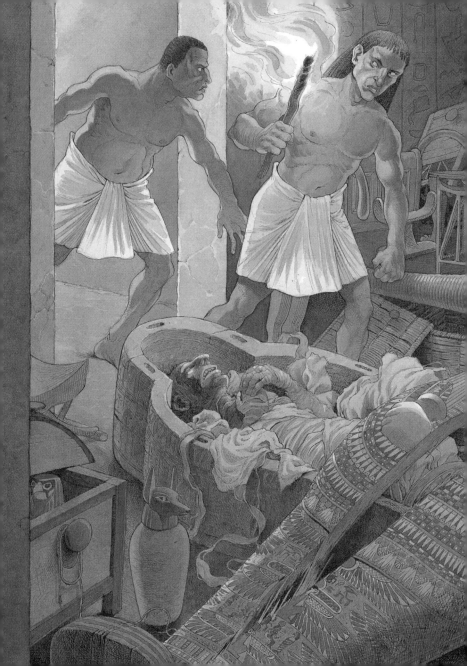

and whispered that we should turn back, but I broke free and followed the lamps down the left tunnel.

Where the narrow corridor grew wider, the scent was overpowering. Tamyt's whispers rose to a shriek, *"Look!"* The burial chamber was in chaos, and the brightly painted coffin lid was split in two. I lit a splinter and held it up. It blazed just long enough for us to glimpse into the coffin at a shiny black face. The tomb robbers had ripped off the mummy's linen strips to get at jewelry bound between them. It was the sweet smell of the funeral ointments that filled the tunnels.

There was another horror to follow: we heard footsteps on the ladder! I grabbed Tamyt, and we scarcely had time to slip into the shadow of another dark chamber before bright torches lit up the tunnel. It was not the robbers returning but the cemetery guards. Tamyt and I thought the guards would search everywhere and find us, but instead the two men merely glanced around, then climbed out. It was as if they had *expected* to discover the robbery.

As soon as they had left, we rushed to the foot of the shaft, but the ladder had gone. We could see its end high above us — far out of reach.

Father came after daybreak. His voice calling our names woke us, and when we replied, he lowered the ladder. We climbed out, and I was sure this time I would get a beating, but instead he just looked tired and relieved.

I sat in front of him as we rode home in our second-best chariot. "When the wind dropped last night, it was too dark to find you on my own," he told us. "I could not ask the guards for help because I should not have been there myself."

I remember no more of what he said, for I fell asleep. Both Tamyt and I had been too afraid to get much sleep as uninvited guests in the underground tomb.

## Fourth day

Today I did not go to school. I stayed home with Tamyt, for Father wanted to know what we had seen at Saqqara.

We told him everything we could remember. When he heard about the three-fingered man and his ring, he urged us to tell him what the ring looked like. I could remember there was an owl carved on it, and a grain store. But there were other signs as well, and no matter how hard I tried, I could not remember what they were. Worse than this, Father asked, "Which finger was missing?" and neither of us knew. Of course, losing a finger is not unusual: few quarrymen have all eight.

Father thanked us for our help, but I could tell that he wished we had noticed more.

## Tenth day

These past days I have been unable to write, for my left arm has been quite useless. Returning from school a few days ago, May and I stopped by the river, where there is a rope hanging from a tree. May swung on the rope and landed nimbly on his feet. Then he challenged me to do the same. I leaped and clung to the rope as he had, and it carried me high into the air. But as I swung back, I lost my grip, and the ground rushed up toward me. I put out my arm, but the ground was stronger and my arm snapped like a twig.

May laughed at first, but when he realized how badly I was hurt, his eyes filled with fear. He helped me home, and as soon as Mother saw me, she sent Ahmose for the Sunu.

Though he does not usually see patients in the afternoon, the Sunu came immediately, for Ahmose made my injuries sound far worse than they really were. Once he had examined me, however, he sighed with relief, saying, "The boy has only a broken arm." Then he commanded Ahmose to cut down a tree branch about one cubit long and a hand thick.

When Ahmose
returned, the Sunu took
the stick and, with a
knife, cut the bark
from it. Then he
poured honey where
my skin was broken
and wrapped the
bark around it.
Finally he tied
the bark up so I
could not move my arm.
While doing all this, he
recited a magic spell to heal me.

Finally the Sunu brought out a tiny jar shaped like
the head of a poppy. He mixed the powder in it with
water and made me sip it. This bitter medicine slowly
made the pain in my head and arm go away and then
sent me to sleep.

## Thirteenth day

To help me write, Tamyt has set out my palette and fetched water for me. There is nothing really worth writing *about*. But for the practice (and because I am so BORED), I will describe the things that go on in the house.

Today I watched Ahmose and the others make bread. They were making a lot, so they kneaded the dough with their feet in a big jar. Ahmose threatened to make me do it. "It is only your arm that is broken," she said, "so your legs can do some work!"

I watched them cook the bread in the oven in the yard. They baked little triangular loaves to offer the gods at a festival and half-baked loaves that they will break up tomorrow to make into beer. We ate some flat loaves that Ahmose had made with dinner.

## Fourteenth day

My arm feels much better. Perhaps writing practice helps it? The women ground wheat today. I had not realized how much time it takes. Each had a turn at the stone, except for the eldest, whose back and knees are worn out from the grinding. Unless one of them works at the stone all the time while the sun shines, there will not be enough flour for tomorrow's bread. To lighten the work, they sang songs and gossiped as they rocked back and forth.

## First day of the third month of the season of Planting

My arm is much improved now and tomorrow is the feast day of Nut. To celebrate, we are going to the Delta for three days' hunting.

## Third day

Though we set off from home before dawn yesterday, we did not arrive here until after dusk. The mosquitoes began feasting on us before we had even moored our boat, and my face already has a million bites.

Today our Uncle Sety took our three cousins, Tamyt, and me to hunt duck. We laid down two framed nets in shallow water. Then we hid, each taking hold of a draw rope. When the birds were over the nets, Sety signaled we should all pull together so the nets clapped over the birds. But we pulled in such a rush we all fell over!

## fourth day

Today we saw a hippopotamus hunt! The people who live here want to kill the beast because it has been destroying their crops. What it does not eat, the hippopotamus tramples flat, so whole fields can be lost in a single night.

The farmers gathered on the bank this morning, having armed themselves with harpoons — spears with cruel hooks at their tips and ropes tied to their ends. We did not dare go too close but followed after them in our wooden boat.

After an hour, we guessed that they had spotted the hippo, for all the hunters suddenly stood upright on their boats and became silent. From a distance, though, we could not see their quarry. All that a sleeping hippo shows above the water are his eyes, ears, and nostrils.

The hunt leader paddled closer, slowly and warily. I held my breath as he raised his harpoon, then hurled it with all his might at the beast. The point glanced off the

hippopotamus's thick hide, which angered him mightily. He opened his vast mouth and let out such a loud roar that, all around us, birds took flight and the air was filled with wing beats and frightened screeches.

The other hunters hurled their harpoons. One managed to thrust his so hard that it stuck in the beast's thick hide. The hippopotamus vanished beneath the water. The man who had speared it tied the harpoon's rope to his boat, but it pulled the boat through the water at such speed the hunter's fear was plain to see. Eventually he was forced to cut the rope. The hunt was over — for today, at least.

## Seventh day of the fourth month of the season of Planting

At school today, May told me his brother has learned that the king's army has just returned from a mighty journey to the land of Punt. He said that the Queen of Punt is so fat that she cannot walk, that the soldiers carried whole ships across the desert and back, that they brought back a mountain of incense, gold, elephant tusks, skins of spotted cats bigger than men, and black wood that is as hard as stone. I might have believed him if the story had not been so fantastic, but it was obviously all lies.

## Ninth day

Tamyt has thought of a brilliant way to find out who the tomb robbers are. She says we should ask the gods. "When there is a festival, the priests carry a god through the street," she reminded me. "You can write a question on a piece of pottery and then, when the priests stop to rest, you can place it before the god. If the answer is yes, the bearers will move forward. If no, they move back."

This seemed like a good idea to me at first, but we could not think of a way to ask our question so the god could answer with a simple yes or no.

Then I remembered that May's brother is a priest

at the temple of the god Ptah. Perhaps if *he* asked the question, Ptah would say more than just yes or no? Tamyt agreed that we should ask, so I wrote on my best, squarest piece of limestone:

"*Great and glorious god Ptah,*
*how can we catch the tomb robbers?*"

I wrapped it in a piece of cloth to give to May.

## Thirteenth day

Yesterday, after school, May took Tamyt and me to meet his brother at the temple. Normally I hurry past the tall gateway, in case the god inside should see me passing and become angry. So when we got there, I was scared at first, but May walked straight in and waved to us to follow. His brother was sitting beyond, in the courtyard. It is HUGE. It seems at least twice as big on the inside as it is outside! Beyond the courtyard, there is a covered area held up by columns. Each is as tall as a palm tree, and much thicker, and there are hundreds of them.

May's brother led us among them, and when my eyes got used to the darkness, I saw colorful carvings on the wall. May whispered that they showed the king worshipping the gods.

When we had walked around once, I asked if our question had been answered. May's brother first said, "I could not ask the god myself, for I am not yet a full priest, so I gave it to one who may approach the god."

"And did he answer?" Tamyt asked.

"Of course. Ptah is all-knowing, but sometimes his replies are puzzling . . ." he said, then paused.

Now I was becoming impatient, too, but did not dare interrupt him again.

"The god answered your question," he said at last, and handed it back to me wrapped in a linen bag. "Ptah says . . . that Anubis, the god of the dead, may not act at once, but those who offend him cannot escape his anger in the end."

As we left the temple, Tamyt and I argued about what

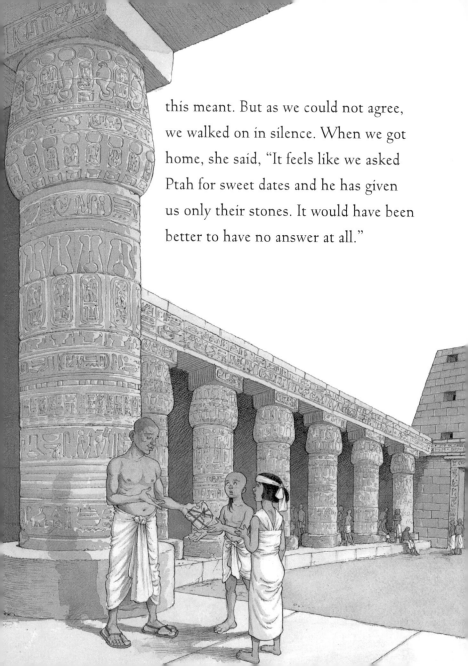

this meant. But as we could not agree, we walked on in silence. When we got home, she said, "It feels like we asked Ptah for sweet dates and he has given us only their stones. It would have been better to have no answer at all."

## Third day of the first month of the season of Heat

Today I saw Father for the first time in three days, for he has been busy organizing the harvest. This year, he says, the god Min has smiled on us. When the harvest yield is safely stored in granaries, nobody need starve — even if the river does not flood for five years in a row.

At school we learned that the assessor scribes work out how much grain each farmer should have grown by using the sizes of the fields that the surveyors measured and the height of the last flood. I asked what would happen if rats stole a farmer's grain and he could not pay what was expected from him. Our teacher told me that he would have to borrow or pay in some other way, or he would get a painful beating on the soles of his feet. I said this was not very fair, but he corrected me: "This is how it has always been done, and anyway, it keeps farmers from hiding the grain and makes sure they are eager to kill any rats that might eat it."

# Twelfth day

Today we went out from the city to meet the Overseer of Fields and to watch the start of the harvest. There was a ceremony to honor the harvest god, Min, and then the Overseer cut the first of the grain in the field. The Overseer is not a fit man, so by the time he had cut just one armful, he was red and sweating. The harvesters teased him, saying, "Go on, cut some more. Don't be shy."

Then they set to work, keeping time with help from a singer and a village girl who played the flute. As the reapers cut, others stacked. Meanwhile the assessor scribes again measured the fields to make sure that the boundary stones had not been moved.

As the villagers harvested each field, they loaded the crops onto the backs of donkeys to take them for threshing.

The threshing floor has a raised circle of baked mud to stop the grain from spreading. Three oxen walk in circles on the crop. Their hooves break the seed heads from their stalks and remove the seeds' tough coats. Women then take the grain for winnowing. They throw the grain in the air and the breeze blows away the useless chaff, and the good grain falls to the ground.

The threshing and winnowing will go on for days, but before sunset there was already a heap of grain taller than I am. The scribes watched as two sacks were filled with great ceremony. Then, with more prayers to Min, they carried the sacks on donkeys back to the city. One sack went into the common granary; the other was stored to sow as seed next planting season.

## Twentieth day

Today the women finished a length of linen that they had been weaving for a month. Tamyt and Mother cut it from the loom and carefully rolled it. They then spent the WHOLE afternoon talking about what they will get in exchange for the cloth. Tamyt wants to barter it for a chair, "So that I do not have to squat on the floor like a servant when we eat." But Mother wants to use it to pay the rent on our fields.

The argument did not end until it was time to prepare dinner, when the two of them were too busy bossing the cooks around (and too hot from the fire) to talk anymore.

## Twenty-second day

This morning I went to the craftsmen's quarter of town, but not with Father. Instead, I followed another scribe, an Overseer of Goldsmiths. He keeps track of the workers who use gold and silver — and those who use copper and bronze, for these metals are scarce too.

At the workshops we visited, he weighed each piece of jewelry and every other object the goldsmiths had made. He had a record of how much metal the craftsmen had received, and with some clever calculation, he judged how much metal had been wasted. "In this way," he told me, "I can be sure that a worker is not taking home even the tiniest shavings of precious gold."

## Twenty-third day

I returned once more to the craftsmen's quarter with the Overseer of Goldsmiths. This time we visited five scorching factories. Everywhere we went there seemed to be a fire pit to melt metal. Beside each one, a filthy boy stood fanning the fire with a foot

bellows until it roared louder than the wind from the desert and burned hotter than the sun. By the last factory, I had decided that overseeing metals was *not* the kind of work I wished to do.

My guide must have noticed my discomfort, for he soon took me to visit some other workshops. In one street alone, we visited painters, potters, workers of leather, and carvers of stone vessels. Each workshop was a surprise, for although I have often seen *what* they make in these places, I have never seen *how* they make it.

We passed quickly through the potters' yard, as this had another searing furnace in it for baking pots. However, we stayed long enough for me to notice that the workers themselves were like living pots: the mud with which they worked covered them from head to foot! I kept glancing at their eyes to remind myself that there were people inside their muddy skins.

The stone-vessel makers were likewise covered, but with dry dust from the rock they cut. This same dust made the older ones cough and spit without ceasing. Their work is the most tiresome of all: to hollow out a jar or bottle, they must turn a drill a million times or more until the walls are thin enough for light to shine through. The outside they shape with bronze chisels. Then they polish the jars with sand and mud.

The tanning yard, which we visited last, was by far the worst. The loudest sound *there* was the buzz of flies, which feed on the fresh animal skins waiting to be treated. I cannot describe the smell. The stench of drying hides mingles with the reek of the urine that fills the pits where they soak and soften. . . . Worst of all, the tanners *walk* in these vats of filth, treading the hides! No wonder their houses are outside the city wall. The smell clung to me so strongly that when I returned home, I was not allowed in the house until I had taken off *all* my clothes and washed from head to toe — twice.

## First day of the second month of Heat

Something so incredible has happened that I cannot make my brush shape the letters fast enough! But I know I must not hurry. Unless I write down everything from the beginning, I will spoil the end of the tale — just as a roast duck spoils if the fire is too hot.

Yesterday began normally enough, but we knew that in the evening the Controller of Granaries would be coming to eat with us. So from the moment the sun rose, Father was asking nervously about the food and other arrangements. After a hundred questions, Tamyt and Mother refused to answer any more, and they bustled off to organize the meal.

This took all day (and indeed, the fussing had begun

a week ago). There was more food than I have ever seen. Besides a delicious ox head, there were birds' eggs and both fresh and pickled fish. Ahmose strangled and plucked some of the ducks in the garden, where they have been fattening ever since we finally trapped them in the Delta.

The Controller of Granaries arrived an hour late. He arrived in a procession fit for a priest. Though Father was furious at his lateness, we all bowed low to him anyway. When we gathered to eat, Father said I had to sit next to him. I thought this very odd, for I normally sit with Tamyt, but Father stared hard at me, as he does only when he is about to be cross, so I sat down.

At dinner, we talked about the tomb robberies. The Controller said that the robbers had killed a man who discovered them at work. When Tamyt heard this, her eyes grew wide with alarm at *our* narrow escape. The conversation ended with Father saying, "Don't worry, sir. I feel we are close to solving the mystery."

The Controller simply nodded with his head down, but he looked up suddenly when Father continued, "The answer has been staring me in the face all the time."

When we were ready to eat fruit, the Controller of Granaries picked up a fig and held it in his left hand to peel it. The light from the lamp fell on his ring, and I saw that it was just like the ring the tomb robber had worn at Saqqara! I jumped up and pointed. "The ring!" I gasped. "It's carved with the same symbols!" The cup I had been holding fell to the floor and smashed, and Mother came and slapped my hand. She pushed me to sit down, hissing, "Now, apologize!" in my ear.

I made an excuse, and the meal went on, but after this slip, I thought the Controller of Granaries looked at me very strangely: never directly, but out of the corner of his eye.

But there was another shock to come. When it was time for the Controller to go, I watched his servants help him down the steps. I gazed at their muscular arms, down to where their big hands gripped their master's arms to assist him. It was then that I noticed that one of them had a finger missing, like the tomb robber we saw at the City of the Dead!

I might have been mistaken about the ring, but this time I was sure. I jumped forward and grabbed the servant's arm, shouting, "It's him! He's a tomb robber!"

Tamyt ran forward to help me, but the robber was quicker. He let go of the Controller of Granaries — who lost his balance and sprawled down the steps — and pushed us roughly away. In a few long bounds, he had reached the garden wall. Without looking to see what lay beyond, he vaulted straight over it and escaped into the street. I ran after him, but his long legs had taken him out of sight even before I heard the gate slam shut behind me.

By the time I got back to the house, everyone was inside again. The Controller sat defiantly on a chair, but his servants stood roped together in a sulky row. To get the city guard to take them away and lock them up, Father had to agree to take the blame for any trouble the Controller might cause *and* promise each guard a fat goose and two cubits of linen.

And so it was that Tamyt and I caught the tomb robbers — in our own house!

## Fourth day of the second month of Heat

Since the arrest of the Controller of Granaries, everyone in Memphis seems to know us. People I have never seen before greet me by name in the street. Strangers stand and point at our house.

## Sixth day

Our house is soon to have a new room! Mother and Father will sleep in it; Tamyt will have their old room, I will move into hers, Ahmose will sleep in my old room, and the wall of her room will be knocked through into the stable. Thus we shall have space for another ass.

# Eighth day

The Vizier, the king's most important official, arrived in Memphis today to question the Controller of Granaries.

Father said that the Controller denied everything at first and angrily demanded to be released. However, he seemed less sure of himself when the Vizier suggested they go to visit his house, which has been sealed since his arrest.

It took a whole day's searching to find the stolen treasures. Indeed they might never have been found if the Vizier had not asked for a drink of water. The sharp-eyed guard who went to the well noticed a scraping of gold on a stone at its edge. Lowering himself on the well rope, he discovered, halfway down, a hidden chamber filled with tomb ornaments.

## Eleventh day

Today I went with Father into the fields to escape the crowds and heat in town. He wanted to see a machine that a farmer had built by the river to bring water to his crops. The name of this machine is *shaduf*, but a better name would be "stork," for it looks just like that bird drinking from the river.

The action of the machine was very simple. The farmer pulled down on the rope to lower the bucket into the water. When it was full, the weight of the lump of clay on the other end lifted the heavy bucket out of the water as if it weighed nothing! Finally the farmer tipped the water into a trough that slopes toward his field.

Our curiosity was soon satisfied, and we sat down in the shade of a tree and discussed the tomb robberies and the Controller of Granaries.

"The robbers broke into only the richest tombs," Father explained, "and when the officials hurried me around Saqqara, I began to suspect they were protecting someone important. When you told me about the short time the guards spent at the tomb, it convinced me that these were not ordinary tomb robbers."

I asked him how he guessed the Controller of Granaries was involved, and he scratched his head thoughtfully. "Well, you said that there were hieroglyphs of an owl and a granary on the tomb robber's ring. Those are the symbols for a controller of granaries. Members of the household might wear them too. Of course, there are several controllers of granaries. But only one of them recently bought a *very* large house, much larger than you would expect for a man of his importance. I knew he wouldn't rob tombs himself, so I guessed he sent his servants. I thought you or Tamyt might recognize the scoundrels again if you could get close enough. So I needed an occasion at which the Controller could show off. I threw a banquet, and sure enough, he brought his whole entourage."

I didn't know what an entourage was, but I didn't want to interrupt.

"I wasn't sure how the evening would unfold," he continued, "but we caught them — even the three-fingered man did not escape the guards for long."

When I asked him what would happen to the Controller, he did not reply but got up and said, "Come, it's cooler now. Let's go home."

## Sixteenth day

Yesterday, the work to extend our house began. The builders started by making bricks. They did this faster than I would have believed possible. One man mixed dirt, straw, and water while two more poured the mixture into wooden molds. Then they knocked out the blocks to dry in the sun.

I was curious to know why they add straw to the mud, so I asked the overseer, Mekhu, what its purpose was. Instead of explaining, he called over one of his men, who led me to a pile of mud that lacked straw. He showed me how to fill a mold (though more of the mud ended up on me than in the brick) and turn it out.

Finally he pressed my hand into the mud to mark the brick as my own, saying, "We would not want to make your bricks part of *our* wall." He told me to return when the bricks were dry.

## Eighteenth day

Early this morning, a grand messenger arrived. Father thought it was an urgent message for him, but to his amazement, the messenger (who wore the king's cartouche) asked for Tamyt and me. He read from a papyrus scroll and informed us that in order to honor our capture of the tomb robbers, we were commanded to appear before the king at Thebes in a month's time! I could not believe it! I hugged Tamyt and rushed out to tell May.

## Twentieth day

Our new room is already half built. The men who were brick-*makers* are now brick-*layers*. They lay the bricks row upon row, fastening them together with more mud. The lowest part of the wall is not of brick but stone, because were it made entirely of mud brick, our whole house would collapse if the river rose too high.

The corners of the walls are made of stone too, as these are most easily damaged. The doorways and window edges are made of squared timber for strength.

## Twenty-first day

*Two* tailors are at work on outfits for our visit to the palace! We shall both wear pleated kilts, and Tamyt will also wear a tunic. She has tried this on already, and complains that it is so tight she can hardly move her legs. We must also wear shoes. Mine made my feet sore, but Ahmose greased the strap between the toes and now they are not so bad.

## Twenty-second day

Yesterday morning, Mekhu's workers carried tree trunks

up from the river and split them in half with wooden wedges. In the cool of the evening (though with much groaning, cursing, and sweating) they lifted the trees to the top of the wall and laid them side by side. Today they covered the logs with palm matting and then with a layer of bricks, sealing it all with a wash of mud.

I know now why bricks need straw. Mekhu put my brick on the ground and beckoned to his heaviest worker to stand on it. The brick crumbled in a moment. Yet it took the weight of two men to crush a brick with straw. "You see," he told me, "apart, mud and straw are like lone soldiers: they are weak. But a properly made brick is stronger than either straw or mud, just as warriors are stronger when they join together as an army."

## Twenty-third day

Our new room is almost complete. Hieroglyphics at
its base spell out, "Mekhu built me," but this is false.
Mekhu sat in the shade drinking palm wine while his
sunburned slaves were working. The builders will lime-
wash the walls brilliant white tomorrow. However, I will
not see the room finished for a month or more because
tomorrow morning, I leave for Thebes with Father and
Tamyt!

## Eighth day of the third month of Heat

At last we are in Thebes! For the boatmen, sailing
upriver against the current is much harder than traveling
downriver. The boatmen were always adjusting the sails
so we could travel as fast as the wind allowed. And this
was NEVER fast enough for me. Sometimes our boat
moved so slowly that people walking on the bank
passed us by.

# Eleventh day

Around dawn this morning, I heard a wild commotion coming from the river. By climbing a palm tree in the garden, I could get a view of the harbor. At first I saw only distant masts, but when the ships came closer, I heard the sound of drums and trumpets, and I realized it must be the king's army returning from Punt, just as May's brother had reported. Tamyt and I slipped out and hurried down to the dockside for a better look.

There we could see nothing, for EVERYONE from the city wanted to do the same. But from the top of a wall, we watched the ships unload. We did not need to ask what was in the first, for as it drew up at the dockside, the smell of myrrh and frankincense was so strong that it overpowered (for a moment at least) the stinking gutters of Thebes.

Next came — in three boats — a forest! I would not have believed this had I not seen it with my own eyes. To the astonishment of all who watched, ten trees of two kinds, complete with roots, were lifted from each boat. (Later I crushed in my hand a leaf that had fallen from one of the trees, and it smelled of myrrh.)

Behind the trees came great lengths of timber, as black as the darkest night, and after that, shining white elephants' teeth — longer than a man is tall. And following these were the skins of spotted cats as big as cattle. Perhaps *some* of what May told me was true.

Last to come ashore were soldiers. Foot soldiers with spears and shields led them. They carried weapons I had not seen before: long, curved, metal war swords, polished to a fine shine. (If farmers had these for cutting barley instead of a row of flint blades, the harvest would take half as long to reap!) Behind them marched black-skinned Nubian archers, carrying their bows unstrung.

Later we found out that we had missed the greatest sight of all! The king himself had been on the far side of the dock to receive the gifts from Punt. We also learned news of this strange and distant place, including the fact

that the Queen of Punt must be carried wherever she goes because she is so fat!

And so I discovered that May did not tell a single lie after all.

# Twelfth day of the third month of Heat

I hardly slept last night, and had to rise TWO HOURS before dawn to wash and dress for our trip to the palace this morning. Though it is only a short walk away, Father was concerned that we would get our new clothes dusty on the way, so he sent for chairs to collect us just after sunrise. Father went in one, and Tamyt and I shared the other. This ride made me feel like a prince, for it was the first time I have ever been carried anywhere in a chair.

Alas, there was hardly time to enjoy it, for we were soon at the palace gates, and then inside. The palace is a little like a temple — but as a temple courtyard is big and airy, so the palace is bigger and airier. Great trees

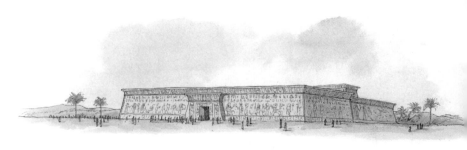

grow in the palace garden, but the walls are so high that
the trees are almost invisible from the outside. There is
water everywhere — in pools and in trickling streams.
The ceilings are so high that you must crane your neck
to look up at them, and gold and brilliant colors cover
everything. But what surprised me most of all was
that — like us — the king lives in a house of mud! I had
expected that the palace would be built of stone, like a
tomb, but it is not. As we rode in, we saw a new wall
being built, and it was made of mud bricks.

Once we were inside the palace, we stood for *hours*
in a long line waiting to see the king, but we stayed cool
under brightly colored linen tents.

While we waited, a courtier told us how to behave
before the king. Nobody is allowed to speak directly to

his face. Even his closest advisers must look away and talk as if he is not there at all. For instance, they do not say, "Do you want me to do this or that?" but, "Does the king wish me to do this or that?"

We learned all this as we moved slowly across an inner courtyard toward the throne. I could see little because there were so many people, but as we drew closer, I spied King Hatshepsut sitting in the shade between two great towering columns.

The first thing I noticed was how thin and small he was. Because he is all-powerful, I had expected to see a bigger man. The king's small size made the crown he wore seem enormous, and his broad gold collar looked especially large below such a slim face.

The long line moved slower than a snail up a reed, but eventually we were close enough to see the king clearly. It was Tamyt who noticed first. . . . Her eyes grew as round as lotus pads. She turned to me and gasped, "The king is a WOMAN!"

I looked carefully, and Tamyt was right. Underneath the false beard and great crown, King Hatshepsut really is a woman!

Father whispered, "Of course! Didn't you realize?" But before I could reply, it was our turn, and we bowed low. A servant read out what we had done, but so quickly I could hardly understand it. Then another official nudged me and muttered, "Move along now." But as he did, the king looked straight at us and held up his — her — hand.

"Wait a minute!" she said to the official, and then to us, "You two have been very clever and brave." She smiled. "Thank you." She nodded and we were hurried away.

It was all over in less time than it takes an ibis to pluck a fish from the water, but the king had *spoken* to us, as if we were viziers, or gods!

## Last day

This past half-month we spent returning to Memphis, so I have not bothered to keep up my journal. When I unroll it now to the beginning and read my words from nearly a year ago, it is hard to believe I was traveling the same river. It seemed so exciting then; this time, I longed for the journey to end. Before the boatmen laid a plank ashore at Memphis, I had leaped onto the dock, and would have run home if Father had not called me to wait for Tamyt.

## Second day of the last month of Heat

When I arrived at school today, all my class threw themselves to the ground, crying, "Hail, Nakht, friend of the king." So it went on, until our teacher told them to show more respect for Hatshepsut and threatened to beat anyone who teased me.

In class we learned how the heaviest stones of Khufu's great pyramid were moved when it was constructed more than 1,000 years ago. It was built during the flood seasons, when work in the fields was impossible. In Khufu's time, it still had a shiny golden top.

## Eleventh day

Yesterday, to celebrate the fact that we had captured the tomb robbers, Father said he would keep his promise and take us to King Khufu's pyramid. The journey is not a special one — we only cross the edge of the desert — but Mother is making a terrible fuss nevertheless. She wants to know if lions are a danger and whether we will have enough water. Anyone would think we were setting out on a journey to Punt.

## Fourteenth day

To travel to Khufu's pyramid, we left before dawn so that we would arrive before the sun became too hot. Idy pulled the chariot because he smells less than the other asses and does not bite.

The pyramid came into sight when we were yet far away. It is so big it is hard to believe it was built by men. Surely only a god could create something so tall and perfectly shaped. Each side is polished so that when we first glimpsed it in the moonlight, the tomb gleamed like ivory. And after dawn, it reflected the sun's rays so brightly, it was painful to look at directly.

To study the pyramid's surface, we had to walk around to the shaded side. Even there, we could scarcely see the joints between the stones. If I did not know better, I would have said it had been carved from a single piece of brilliant white rock.

The entrance to the tomb is high up on one side. There is a stone door that lifts up. When it closes, the doorway is completely invisible. We decided not to enter, but other visitors, who had less respect for Khufu's spirit, bought torches from guides, climbed up, and went inside. They returned disappointed, and told us that the tunnel slopes down to a filthy cellar full of rats and flying mice.

The guides who sell torches also sell countless other things. Many sell beer, and even water; others offer to draw a quick portrait of visitors; more still sell cheap trinkets. All of them charge at least double what their goods are worth. These men crowded around us when we arrived, and clung to us like leeches until they found another visitor to pester.

We had arrived
at the pyramids at
dawn, and by the
time we were ready
to leave, the sun was
scorching our backs.

On our way home, we passed
the vast stone head of a king. Father said that hidden
beneath the sand, the statue has the body of a lion.
Though he swore this is so, neither Tamyt nor I
believed him.

My final treat was to drive home. Father gave me the
reins, and we raced across the edge of the desert so fast
that Tamyt begged me to slow down because she feared
she would be thrown from the chariot.

## Sixteenth day

Father announced today that I am to lose my sidelock at
the next full moon. I will no longer be a child!

## Twenty-third day of the last month of Heat

I found out at last what had happened to the Controller of Granaries. I thought he would be put to death, but his punishment was worse than this. His nose was cut off, he was banished to a quarry in the desert to work as a slave, and (worst of all) his name has been taken away. Without a name, he no longer exists — and never has — so no one speaks of him in Memphis anymore.

## Twenty-ninth day

Yesterday I became a man! Though if I had known how much fuss there was going to be about a haircut, I think I would have chosen to remain a child for longer. First I had to lead a procession around the neighborhood, inviting everyone to our house. Then, when they were all sitting in a circle in the garden, I crouched in the middle. Father brought out a stone knife sharp enough to use as a razor. He cut my sidelock — not all at once, but a little at a time, according to the gifts that everyone gave me. If it was a large gift, like the goat my uncle promised, he cut off half a palm's width. For the smallest gifts, such as the honey cake and fruit that my friends had brought, he trimmed just the ends of a few hairs.

When it was all cut and my head shaved, I put on a white robe with a green apron, and Tamyt led *another* procession. May and most of my class walked behind, carrying palm branches. At each house, we stopped and chanted, and at each one, they brought out gifts of food. Finally we all returned home, and Mother made a meal with the gifts we had collected.

It was a great party, but everyone teased me about losing my sidelock. I soon tired of them patting my shaved head where it had hung. When musicians came and the dancing began, people no longer came to congratulate me, and I slipped away to my bed. As I fell asleep, I noticed that the music did not stop, so nobody missed me!

## First day of the first month of the season of flood

This morning, the star Sopdet reappeared at dawn, marking the start of the new year, the ninth of our great King Hatshepsut — may she live forever!

# Nakht's World

# Where Was Ancient Egypt?

Ancient Egyptian civilization grew up on the banks of the lower Nile River, at the top right-hand corner of Africa. It stretched roughly five hundred miles south from the Delta region, where the river flows into the Mediterranean Sea.

Egypt's great river gave life to the country. It watered the crops; its rich mud did the same job as the fertilizers that modern farmers spread on their fields; and it was a transport super-highway, along which travelers and merchandise could float effortlessly the whole length of their country.

The Nile flooded so regularly that the Egyptians based their calendar on its rising and falling waters.

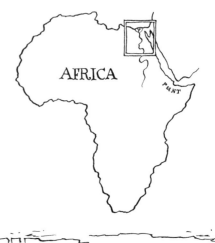

AFRICA

PUNT

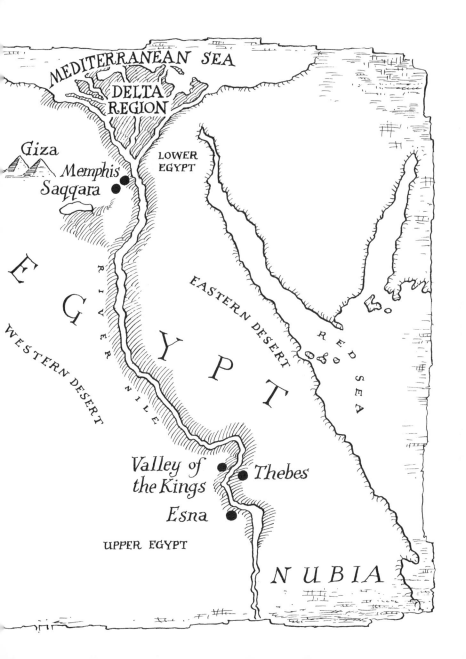

 THOUGH NAKHT'S DIARY is a fictional story, his descriptions of Ancient Egypt are true to life. Hatshepsut really did rule Egypt 3,500 years ago (one of only three native female kings in Ancient Egyptian history), and corrupt officials often let tomb robbers escape justice. However, Nakht's story touches on only a tiny part of a civilization that flourished on the banks of the Nile for more than 5,000 years.

# Nakht's World
## What Do We know?

What we know about Ancient Egypt comes from objects that archaeologists have found buried and from ancient writings on documents, monuments, and tombs.

Egypt is a desert. The air is very dry, and away from the Nile, the ground is parched. The dryness has preserved objects buried in the sand and in tombs cut into the rock or built from stone and brick.

However, the banks of the Nile were the center of most of life in Ancient Egypt. These areas flooded each year, and the water destroyed many of the objects that archaeologists would love to study.

# What Survived?

The part of Ancient Egyptian life that we know a great deal about is death. The ancient Egyptians attached huge importance to it. They went to a lot of trouble to preserve the bodies of the dead and performed elaborate ceremonies in their honor. Inscriptions on tomb walls and in special Books of the Dead explain these rituals in minute detail.

Fortunately, one particular part of the Egyptian obsession with death has helped archaeologists in their struggle to re-create the past: the custom of burying along with the dead the things they might need in the afterlife (see pages 106–107). Since people believed that the needs of the dead were not very different from the needs of the living, tombs were stacked with furniture, food, and many other personal objects — or with models of these things.

So tombs are a major source of information about ancient everyday life.

# The Rosetta Stone

The inscriptions that archaeologists study on tomb walls are mostly written in hieroglyphics — a form of picture writing. But for many years they had no idea what the pictures represented. The meaning of the hieroglyphics remained a mystery until the end of the 1700s and the discovery of a stone at the Egyptian town of Rosetta. This unique stone was inscribed with hieroglyphics *and* with Greek and demotic (another Egyptian script). Archaeologists could read Greek and soon realized that all three inscriptions said the same thing. They had cracked the code and could now begin to translate hieroglyphic and demotic writing accurately.

# Cracking the Code

*Here is a sentence written in hieroglyphics, demotic script, and Greek. There are no spaces between the words. In English, it means:* **Lions ate my gardener**

*Hieroglyphics (read from left to right)*

*Demotic (read from right to left)*

ΟΙΛΕΩΝΤΕΣΕΦΑΓΟΝΤΟΝΕΜΟΝΚΗΠΟΥΡΟΝ

*Ancient Greek (read from left to right)*

# Egyptian Society

Ancient Egyptian society was organized like a pyramid. At the very tip was the king. The king was always a man — even when "he" was a woman.

Hatshepsut is shown dressed in the same way as male kings, even wearing a false beard.

The Egyptians believed the king was not just their ruler but also a god. They believed that the king's power had no limits and that he knew and controlled everything, including the natural world.

It was the king's job to look after all Egypt's people. He was in charge of the army, the courts and justice system, the temples and religion.

Supporting the king was a small group of officials. Many of them were relatives of the king. These people made up the Egyptian nobility.

Below these noblemen were scribes, like Nakht's father. Scribes weren't as wealthy as the nobles, but they were well off.

Scribes did everything needed to keep the country running, including collecting taxes, enforcing the law, and arranging for food handouts when there was a famine. Each scribe was a specialist who took care of one specific kind of task.

At these two high levels in the pyramid of power, there were also religious officials — priests and high priests — who organized the many temple rituals and ceremonies.

Lower in status than the scribes and priests were Egypt's craftsmen. These skilled workers created the fine ornaments and luxury goods that the king and those around him used. There were more craftsmen than scribes, but the craftsmen were hugely outnumbered by those beneath *them* — Egypt's peasant farmers.

Much of what the farmers produced was paid to the king in taxes — so their grain or livestock went to feed the scribes, priests, and nobility.

At the very bottom of the pyramid were the slaves. They acted as household servants or farm laborers. Many slaves were foreigners, captured in battle by Egypt's armies. Others were Egyptians who had sold themselves into slavery to pay off debts. It wasn't just rich scribes or nobles who owned slaves — even common Egyptians could afford them.

# Who Was Who in Ancient Egypt

King

Nobility

Scribes

Craftsmen

Farmers

Slaves

# The Gods

Egyptians worshipped many gods, but not all had equal status. The least important were house gods, some of whom had special responsibilities or guarded against particular dangers.

More important state gods had temples dedicated to them, where priests performed rituals in their honor. These gods kept disorder and chaos at bay. The Egyptians were so concerned about leading proper, well-ordered lives that they even had a word for it: *maat*. Though it's impossible to translate into a single English word, *maat* means the right way to do things; order, freedom from chaos; truth and balance. Egyptian people valued *maat* very highly, and it was important to respect the gods in order to preserve *maat*.

### ◀ AMUN-RE

Before Hatshepsut's time, the sun god, Re, merged with another god, Amun. The new god, Amun-Re, was the king of Egypt's gods.

### ANUBIS ▶

The god of the dead, Anubis guarded mummies.

### ◀ HAPY

Egyptians believed Hapy was responsible for the Nile's annual floods.

### ISIS ▶

The goddess Isis was worshipped for her protective power, particularly her ability to guard children.

◀ KHNUM

The guardian of the source of the Nile.

▲ NUT

The sky goddess,

Nut was usually shown stretching over the world,
with her hands and feet touching the earth.

◀ OSIRIS

The god of death, but also of fertility
and rebirth. His death and resurrection
came to stand for the annual cycle of
crop growth.

### ◀ PTAH

The local guardian god of Memphis,
he was believed to have shaped all living
beings on a potter's wheel and was
the protector of craftspeople.

### SOBEK ▶

In Egyptian myth, the Nile's waters
were made from the sweat of this
crocodile god.

### ◀ THOTH

Shown as either a baboon
or an ibis, Thoth was the god of
writing and knowledge.

# Life after Death

The need for *maat* did not end with death, for Egyptians believed in an afterlife. The afterlife could last forever, but only if the dead person's family performed all the right rituals, filled the tomb with the correct equipment, and, most important of all, took care to preserve the body.

## Mummies

*To keep the body from rotting, it was dried out and treated with naturally occurring chemicals, then wrapped in linen strips to form a mummy. There were simple, cheap forms of mummification, as well as more elaborate methods for those who could afford them. In the best and costliest version . . .*

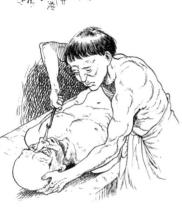

1. The embalmers scooped out the brains using an iron hook.

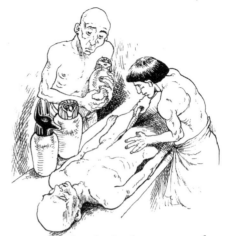

2. With a flint knife, they cut open the body and removed the internal organs, storing them in special containers called canopic jars.

3. They washed the body cavity with spices and palm wine, then covered it in dry natron — a natural salt found in the desert. The chemicals soaked up all the liquids from the body, preventing decay.

4. After seventy days, the embalmers stuffed the empty body, wrapped the mummy, and put it into a human-shaped coffin for burial.

# Tombs

After elaborate funeral ceremonies, Egyptian people buried the mummified corpse. Those who could afford it dug an underground tomb big enough to contain the coffin and other equipment needed on the journey to the afterlife. Above it, they constructed a kind of chapel, where living relatives could pray and make offerings to the dead.

# Pyramids

The grandest of all memorials to the dead were the pyramids. Pyramid building began about 4,700 years ago. By the time it ended, 1,000 years later (around 200 years before Nakht was born), there were eighty or so pyramids on the desert's edge on the west bank of the Nile.

# Robbers

Pyramids protected the precious objects entombed with the kings inside but weren't as secure as modern safes and strong rooms. All were robbed eventually.

Tomb robbers forced Egypt's rulers to look for better ways of protecting their dead, and they eventually decided that secrecy was the answer. By about 1500 BC they had begun cutting tombs into rock cliffs in the Valley of the Kings, near Thebes, and then building funeral chapels some distance away.

Even these hidden graves were often robbed, but one, the tomb of Tutankhamun (1336–1327 BC) escaped complete destruction. When it was opened in the early twentieth century, the fabulous gold treasures found inside astonished the world.

# Khufu's Pyramid

The grandest of all the pyramids is the one built for Khufu (2589–2566 BC) at Giza. Usually called the Great Pyramid, it is constructed from huge blocks of stone, some weighing as much as fifteen tons.

Khufu's pyramid contains more mysterious tunnels and chambers than any other, including a sloping corridor pointing to the stars.

### KEY

1 ENTRANCE
2 DESCENDING CORRIDOR
3 UNDERGROUND CHAMBER
4 SERVICE CORRIDOR
5 ASCENDING CORRIDOR
6 QUEEN'S ROOM
7 GREAT GALLERY
8 AIR SHAFTS

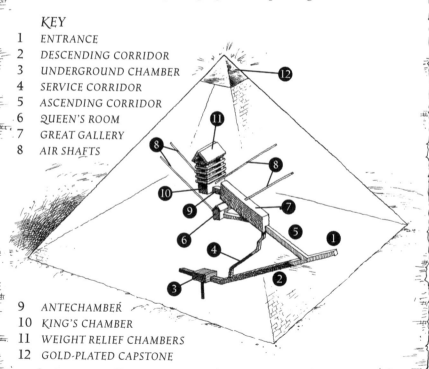

9 ANTECHAMBER
10 KING'S CHAMBER
11 WEIGHT RELIEF CHAMBERS
12 GOLD-PLATED CAPSTONE

# Glossary
## and Index

# Glossary and Index

Page numbers that are <u>underlined</u> show where terms connected with Ancient Egyptian life are explained in the text. Other unusual words are explained here. Words shown in *italics* have their own entries, with more information or pages to look up.

# C

CANALS 22–23

CARGO 29

CARPENTERS 11

CARTOUCHES 70
Hieroglyphics encased in an oval shape that show royal or divine names.

CARVINGS 49

CHARIOTS 37, 83, 85

CITY OF THE DEAD 5, 7, 24, 32 A piece of ground set aside for burial, like a cemetery.

CLOTHING 3, 15, 19, 28, 71, 79, 87. See also *shoes*

COFFINS 19, 24, 36, 107, 108

COOKS 12, 54

CONTROLLER OF GRANARIES 14–15, 58–65, 67–68, 86

CRAFTSMEN 54–55, 100

CROCODILES 26, 27

CUBITS 25, 39 A unit of measurement that matched the length of the king's arm from his elbow to the tip of his middle finger.

# D

DANCERS 17

DELTA 43, 59, 92

# E, F

EMBALMERS 107

ENTOURAGE 68
A group of attendants.

ESNA 1, 6, 10, 12

FARMING 22–25, 44, 51–53, 66–67 See also *harvest*

FOOD 3, 4–5, 12, 19, 21, 58–59, 87, 96, 99

FUNERALS 17, 108

FURNITURE 19, 33, 96

# M

# N

# O

OVERSEER OF

# P

# R

# Sources

Writers and illustrators owe a debt of gratitude to the authors and artists whose works inspire them. Richard Platt and David Parkins are especially grateful, because they searched in more than forty books for details that would make the text and pictures authentic. There isn't room to list them all, but the following are among the more recently published books.

Andreu, Guillemette: Egypt in the Age of the Pyramids

El Mahdy, Christine: Mummies, Myth and Magic in Ancient Egypt

Filer, Joyce: Egyptian Bookshelf: Disease

Gill, Anton: Ancient Egyptians

Janssen, Rosalind M. & Jac J.: Growing Up in Ancient Egypt

Partridge, Robert: Transport in Ancient Egypt

Sandison, David: The Art of Egyptian Hieroglyphics

Shaw, Ian & Paul Nicholson: **British Museum Dictionary of Ancient Egypt**

Strouhal, Eugen: **Life of the Ancient Egyptians**

Tyldesley, Joyce: **Hatshepsut, the Female Pharaoh**

Unstead, R. J.: **How They Lived in Cities Long Ago**

Vercoutter, Jean: **The Search for Ancient Egypt**

Wilkinson, Alix: **The Garden in Ancient Egypt**

RICHARD PLATT has been fascinated by Ancient Egypt ever since he first saw the leathery face of a mummy in the British Museum. He has written more than ninety books, including *Roman Diary*, *Castle Diary*, which won the Kate Greenaway Medal, and *Pirate Diary*, which won the Nestlé Smarties Children's Book Prize Silver Medal and a Blue Peter Book Award. Richard Platt lives with his wife, cat, and five chickens in Kent, England.

DAVID PARKINS has illustrated numerous books for children, including picture books, poetry, fiction, and nonfiction. He is the illustrator of *Roman Diary*, also written by Richard Platt. David Parkins lives in Canada with his family and three cats.

# CASTLE DIARY

## The Journal of Tobias Burgess, Page

In 1285, eleven-year-old Toby Burgess is sent to be a page in his uncle's castle. While there, he keeps a detailed journal of everything that happens, from boar hunts and tournaments to baking bread and cleaning out toilets! Read Toby's diary and discover the triumphs — and tribulations — of life in a medieval castle.

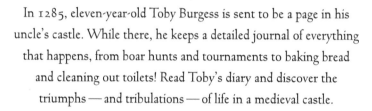

Highly Commended for the Kate Greenaway Medal

Short-listed for the Kurt Maschler Award

A National Council for the Social Studies Notable Trade Book for Young People

A Parents' Choice Recommended Title

A Junior Library Guild Selection

★ "Not many, if any, children's books on the Middle Ages and castles contain the wealth of information found in this fresh, appealing offering." — *School Library Journal* (starred review)

"An informative and amusing introduction to the medieval world." — *Publishers Weekly*

# Pirate Diary

## THE JOURNAL OF JAKE CARPENTER, CABIN BOY

Beginning in 1716, *Pirate Diary* recounts the adventures of nine-year-old Jake Carpenter as he discovers the thrills and perils of life on the high seas. Read Jake's journal about how he takes part in a daring treasure raid, endures a terrifying storm, and learns all about life under the pirate code!

Winner of the Kate Greenaway Medal

A Nestlé Smarties Children's Book Prize
Silver Medal Winner

"Oodles of information on everything from articles of piracy to navigation by dead reckoning is effortlessly incorporated, and Riddell's ink-and-watercolor pictures are both convincingly detailed and deliciously overdrawn."
— *Bulletin of the Center for Children's Books*

★ "Kids looking for adventure will certainly find plenty of it here."
— *School Library Journal* (starred review)

# ROMAN DIARY

## THE JOURNAL OF ILIONA, YOUNG SLAVE

Iliona never imagined that her sea voyage from Greece to Egypt would lead to Rome, but when she is captured by pirates and auctioned off as a slave, that's where she lands. Read Iliona's journal to view the wonders of Rome through her eyes — the luxury, the excess, the politics.

A National Council for the Social Studies
Notable Trade Book for Young People

A Bank Street College Best Children's Book of the Year

An Oppenheim Toy Portfolio Platinum Award Winner

A Junior Library Guild Selection

"Holds readers' attention while presenting characters from various aspects of Roman life. . . . Truthful to history." — *School Library Journal*

"The text is wonderful, rich, and interesting."
— *Lower Columbia Review Group*